Dear mouse friends,
Welcome to the world of

Geronimo Stilton

Geronimo Stilton
A learned and brainy
mouse; editor of
The Rodent's Gazette

Thea Stilton
Geronimo's sister and
special correspondent at
The Rodent's Gazette

Trap Stilton
An awful joker;
Geronimo's cousin and
owner of the store
Cheap Junk for Less

Benjamin Stilton
A sweet and loving
nine-year-old mouse;
Geronimo's favorite
nephew

Geronimo Stilton

MOUSE IN SPACE!

Scholastic Inc.

No part of this publication may be reproduced, stored in a retrieval system, or transmitted in any form or by any means, electronic, mechanical, photocopying, recording, or otherwise, without written permission from the copyright holder. For information regarding permission, please contact: Atlantyca S.p.A., Via Leopardi 8, 20123 Milan, Italy; e-mail foreignrights@atlantyca.it, www.atlantyca.com.

ISBN 978-0-545-48191-5

Copyright © 2011 by Edizioni Piemme S.p.A., Corso Como 15, 20154 Milan, Italy.

International Rights © Atlantyca S.p.A.

English translation © 2013 by Atlantyca S.p.A.

GERONIMO STILTON names, characters, and related indicia are copyright, trademark, and exclusive license of Atlantyca S.p.A. All rights reserved. The moral right of the author has been asserted.

Based on an original idea by Elisabetta Dami.

www.geronimostilton.com

Published by Scholastic Inc., 557 Broadway, New York, NY 10012. SCHOLASTIC and associated logos are trademarks and/or registered trademarks of Scholastic Inc.

Stilton is the name of a famous English cheese. It is a registered trademark of the Stilton Cheese Makers' Association. For more information, go to www.stiltoncheese.com.

Text by Geronimo Stilton
Original title *S.O.S. C'e un topo nello spazio!*
Cover by Giuseppe Ferrario (design) and Giulia Zaffaroni (color)
Illustrations by Francesco Barbieri (design) and Christian Aliprandi (color)
Graphics by Chiara Cebraro

Special thanks to Kathryn Cristaldi
Translated by Lidia Morson Tramontozzi
Interior design by Kay Petronio

12 11 10 9   15 16 17/0

Printed in the U.S.A.   40
First printing, January 2013

TWO CHEESEBRAINS IN BLACK MASKS

It was a dark, chilly, moonless night, and I was snoring **contentedly** under my cozy comforter. I was having the most **fabumouse** dream! In my dream I was floating in space, happily **hovering** over cream cheese asteroids, Swiss cheese planets, and mozzarella comets.

Just as I was about to **nibble** on a yummy-looking cheese crater, **something** woke me up. I heard a **CLICK**, like the sound of a lock being broken. Then I heard a **creak**, like the sound of a door opening. And finally, I heard a **swoosh, swoosh**, like the sound of muffled feet. . . .

Holey cheese! Someone was in my house!

In a panic, I grabbed something to protect myself. Unfortunately, it wasn't a **BASEBALL BAT**. It was my **slipper**. Rats! Still, I forced myself to scamper into the living room. And that's when I saw them. Two shadows in the dark . . .

Wh-who's there?

"**Aaaaah!**" I yelled.

"**Aaaaaaaaah!**" yelled the shadows.

"**AAAAAAAAAAAAAAAAAAH!**"

I yelled louder.

I was so scared, my heart was racing. The SHADOWS were looking more like mice wearing masks. WHO were these intruders? WHAT did they want? Money? Jewelry? A homemade Swiss cheese sandwich on rye?

I'd have to wait to find out. A moment later I fainted.

Clunk!

I woke up the following morning

when a **ray** of sun hit me in the eyes.

With a groan I sat up. Then I rubbed my head, where an **ENORMOUSE** lump had formed.

"Who am I? Where am I? What time is it? Why aren't I in my bed? And why do I have an enormouse **lump** on my head?" I muttered.

Then I tried my best to answer myself.

"Well, um, my name is Stilton, *Geronimo Stilton*. I'm the editor of *The Rodent's Gazette*, the most famous newspaper on Mouse Island. I'm in my house, and it's morning," I answered.

I **SIGHED** with relief. At least the **lump** on my head hadn't turned me completely clueless!

Enormouse lump!

Youch!

A few seconds later, everything came rushing back to me: the two shadows *sneaking* around my house the night before . . . grabbing my slipper . . . **FAINTING**. Had anything been stolen?

I ran to check on Hannibal, my **little red fish**. I gave him some of his favorite food, and he slapped his tail in greeting.

He was as *frisky* and *cheerful* as ever.

Then I checked my collection of **antique cheese rinds**. I'm very fond of them because I found each rind, one by one, in antique shops all over New Mouse City.

Not one was missing. Phew!

I began **opening** drawers and cabinets to make sure everything was where it should be. Carefully, I

pawed through it all — my favorite books, my ties, a **cheddar**-colored sweater from my aunt Sweetfur, a **PAINTED** rock from my dear nephew Benjamin.

Luckily, everything was in its place.

I was so happy. The **intruders** didn't take any of the things that meant the most to me. I didn't really care about my money — but even that was all there, in my wallet, on a table in the living room.

How **odd**!

If nothing was stolen, then what did those two cheesebrains in **black masks** want? Why did they run off?

Suddenly, it dawned on me what had happened. When I held up my slipper and **screamed**, I had scared them away!

That's right — I, *Geronimo Stilton*, biggest **SCAREDY-MOUSE** on all of Mouse

Island, had sent those **rotten** cheesebrains running!

I couldn't believe it. I was a true **HERO**!

I couldn't wait to tell everyone! I **scampered** to the bathroom and began getting ready for work, happily *whistling* to myself.

What a hero!

I looked at myself in the mirror. Yes, I decided, I did look stronger, and prouder. In fact, you could say I looked **heroic**!

I was so busy staring at myself in the mirror that I hadn't heard the phone **ringing**. I picked up after the tenth **ring**. It was my grandfather William Shortpaws.

"GRANDSON! What are you doing?

Why didn't you pick up the phone sooner? I refuse to be kept waiting! Get your tail in gear **PRONTO**! There were a ton of robberies in the city last night!" he *SCREECHED*.

"I know, Grandfather. Last night two cheesebrains in **black masks** broke into my house, too. But I chased them away with a slipper! Oh, and then I fainted. But still, I was a real **HERO**!" I squeaked.

Grandfather snorted.

"A *slipper*? Sure, those slippers can be very scary. Now listen, **HERO**, get your fuzzy head out of your fairy-tale book and get moving. We need to get the scoop on those robberies for the paper. I sent your sister, Thea, over to you with **precise** instructions. You need to figure out who's behind all these robberies. After you do that, write an ace article and have it on my desk by tomorrow morning! Got it? **NOW MOVE IT!**" he shrieked.

I tried to interrupt, but Grandfather wasn't listening.

"**cheese niblets!**" he continued. "If it weren't for me, *The Rodent's Gazette* would be a complete mess! That's right, I'll tell you who the hero is! It's **me! me! me! me!**"

The next thing I heard was the dial tone.

Argh!

CRUNCH!

I stared at the phone, feeling like my grandfather had burst my bubble. Oh, why could I never **IMPRESS** Grandfather William? I made up my mind that this time I was going to show him what kind of a mouse I really was! I'd write an article that was **incredible**, worthy of a prestigious editorial award — the **Best tHing** ever written! Well, okay, maybe not the best thing ever written, but you get the idea. It would be great!

While I waited for my sister to arrive, I showered, dressed, and began to make myself breakfast.

I opened the cabinet and took out a box of **frosted cheesy flakes** and some blue-cheese yogurt. Yum! Then I decided to treat myself to one of the delicious **cream cheese** breakfast cookies I buy for special occasions.

Crunch!

As my mouth watered, I stuck my paw in the jar and pulled out a cookie. Then I took a bite and — **crunch!** — I nearly broke my tooth! So much for soft cheese! Hidden in the middle of the cookie was a **STRANGE** metallic capsule, which held a **STRANGE** note inside.

The **note** was signed by my secret agent friend **OOK**, but it was addressed to somebody named **OOG**.

Message for OOG:
Get ready!
Signed,
OOK

PS: Swallow the note after reading this message! (Don't worry, it's made of sugar!)

OOK

NAME: Kornelius von Kickpaw

CODE NAME: OOK

PROFESSION: Secret agent for the government of Mouse Island

WHO HE IS: Geronimo's friend from elementary school

HOW HE BECAME A SECRET AGENT: No one actually knows how Kornelius became a secret agent. To the rest of Mouse Island, he is simply a wealthy mouse who loves art and racing cars. In reality, he works undercover, leading dangerous missions throughout the world!

ACCESSORIES: He always wears a super-accessorized tuxedo and sunglasses — even at night!

INTERESTING FACT: He always finds bizarre and mysterious ways to communicate because he doesn't want his messages to get intercepted.

OOG

NAME: Geronimo Stilton

CODE NAME: OOG

PROFESSION: Publisher of *The Rodent's Gazette* and part-time secret agent

HOW HE BECAME A SECRET AGENT: When the Mouse Island Secret Service Organization (M.I.S.S.O.) found out someone was planning to steal the Super Mouse Cup golf trophy, they used Geronimo to help catch the thief. Geronimo did such a great job cracking the case, he was made a secret agent.

INTERESTING FACT: He is a complete scaredy-mouse, and often faints when he's in danger. He's afraid of the dark, fast cars, and those paw dryers in public bathrooms (they're so loud!).

My friend must have made a mistake.

PERPLEXED, I muttered to myself, "Who's **00G**? I don't know anyone named 00G."

Then all of a sudden it **HIT** me. *I was* **00G!** A while ago, I had been involved in an adventure with 00K where I was made a secret agent.* **00G** was my code name. How could I have forgotten that?

Immediately, I began to panic. What kind of mission did Kornelius have in mind this time? Was it **DANGEROUS**? Would I make it out alive?

Suddenly, my sister, Thea, **burst** into my kitchen. (Oh, why did I give her my house keys?) Quickly, I shoved the note in my mouth and began chewing. It really was made of sugar! But it was **sticky** and hard to eat.

"Mmf . . . ssmmmr . . . soorr . . ." I mumbled.

* Do you remember? It happened in my adventure *The Giant Diamond Robbery*.

"Gerry, are you okay? You're acting **WEIRD**," Thea said.

I swallowed. "S-s-sorry . . . the sugar . . . I mean, the note . . . I mean, the secret . . ." I babbled.

Thea looked at me strangely. "Okay, listen, Gerrykins, I don't have time for any of your **QUIRKS** today!" she squeaked. "Last night there were oodles of robberies in New Mouse City. And they were all done by the same two **CHEESEBRAINS IN BLACK MASKS**. . . ."

She stuck a photo under my snout. I squeaked.

"I recognize them! They tried to rob my house, too! But I chased them away with my *slipper*!"

"Your *slipper*? Strange," remarked Thea. "But good for you, Gerry Berry. I always thought you were a total scaredy-mouse. That's something a real **HERO** would do. **TOO BAD**, though . . ." Her voice trailed off.

"**TOO BAD** what?" I squeaked.

Thea didn't answer. She was nibbling one of my cream cheese breakfast cookies.

I started to feel worried as Thea chewed and chewed and chewed.

Finally, I couldn't take it anymore. "**TOO BAD** what?!?" I screeched.

Thea swallowed and patted her mouth

with a napkin. Finally, she said, "TOO BAD those two crooks will probably come back to your place to finish off the job. If I were you, Gerrykins, I'd sleep with one EYE open tonight!"

Instantly, I felt sick. "Moldy mozzarella! Now I probably won't be able to SLEEP at all tonight!" I squeaked.

"Good idea," Thea agreed. "Now you'd better get to work. Grandfather wants you to write a **Ratitzer Prize**-winning article for the paper. I've already got the headline: *Hero Geronimo Stilton Chases Away Cheesebrains!*"

After Thea left, I sat down at my computer. But I couldn't concentrate. I kept thinking of those two thugs in **black masks**. Would they come back tonight? Would they be mad? Would I **LIVE** to tell the tale?

Before I knew it, I was shaking. Some hero I was!

Absentmindedly, I stared out the window. That's when I noticed something odd: Overnight, **ENORMOUSE** billboards had sprung up everywhere. There was even one right in front of my window.

Who would need an antitheft device? I thought. Then I **HIT** my forehead. I did! I dialed the number for **SAFE SQUEAK**.

I was greeted by a **recorded** message.

"We are out of the office installing **SAFE SQUEAK** antitheft devices. Please leave a message. Your call will be returned faster than you can say *squeak!*"

I left a message:

"My name is *Geronimo Stilton*. I'm interested in having an antitheft device installed. Please call me back as soon as possible. . . ."

WHAT SERVICE!

I hadn't even finished squeaking when there was a knock at my door. I opened it and saw a **TALL**, slender rodent with **long** blond fur, a dark suit, and **Mysterious** black sunglasses.

I noticed a **SAFE SQUEAK** pin on her jacket, and below it, in small print, the name **Suzy Slyrat**.

I was stunned! What service! Safe Squeak really was *FAST*!

I welcomed Suzy Slyrat and showed her into the living room. She gave me the most mesmerizing smile, then showed me a comprehensive catalog with the most sophisticated antitheft devices I'd ever seen.

"You were so **SMART** to call us, Mr. Stilton," she said in a soothing voice, patting my paw. "But of course, I can already tell you are a **SUPERSMART** mouse. Tonight you'll sleep like a log. We'll keep everything under control with our SUPER-SATELLITE antitheft devices. No thieves will get into your house again. And . . . because you're our one-thousandth customer, you will receive three pieces of equipment for the price of two!"

In less than ten minutes, Miss Slyrat

Done!

convinced me to buy **everything** in the catalog — for a **FUR-RAISING** amount of money!

Half-dazed, I repeated over and over again, "Of course, Miss Slyrat. Thank you, Miss Slyrat. Do what you think is best, Miss Slyrat. . . ."

For some reason I just couldn't say no to such a CHARMING mouse.

"You'll sleep like a **mouseling** tonight, Mr. Stilton, just you **wait** and see!" she insisted as I handed over my **ENORMOUSE** check.

When I finished signing the contract, she grabbed the paper and quickly put it away. She made a phone call, and in less than two minutes, a team of **SAFE SQUEAK** workers took over my house.

This is what they installed: **75 infrared sensors** (on the windows and doors, as well as on the cabinets and refrigerator doors!), **93 detectors** that would sense the presence of any living thing in the building, **38 CAMERAS** (at least 3 in every room!), **1 SECURITY DOOR**, **13 ELECTRIFIED SUPER-REINFORCED SHUTTERS**, and **7 huge eardrum-splitting alarms** (linked to everything).

Any mouse who wanted to get into my house now had to undergo:

- Digital pawprint recognition
- Examination of fur (color and softness incorporated with antiflea treatment)
- Measurement of tail length
- Complete examination of whiskers
- Squeak recognition

ANTITHEFT DEVICES
INSTALLED IN MY HOUSE

1) Infrared sensors
2) Motion and movement detectors
3) Video cameras
4) Security door
5) Electrified titanium super-reinforced shutters
6) Giant earsplitting alarms

1) Track every movement!

2) Also zap bugs on contact!

3) Record everything that happens . . . everywhere!

4) Senses every vibration!

5) Quiet, reliable, and absolutely shatterproof!

6) So loud it can be heard even by ears stuffed with cheese!

The entire system was connected via satellite to **SAFE SQUEAK** headquarters, where a system expert manned the system **24-7**.

When they left, night had fallen. I quickly wrote my article for *The Rodent's Gazette* and **emailed** it in. I advised all of New Mouse City's residents to install some sort of **ANTITHEFT DEVICE** to keep thieves away. Then, completely exhausted, I ate a **COLD** cheese sandwich and headed off to bed.

I'm soooo sleepy....

RANCID RAT HAIRS, THAT MOUSE WAS ME!

I fell asleep instantly. With my new security system I felt supersafe. Nothing would disturb me.

Boy, was I **wrong**! At 11:00 P.M., one of the earsplitting alarms went off:

Terrified, I crept out to my living room. Were the thieves back?

No, it was just my fish, Hannibal. His hiccups had triggered the alarm!

CHEESE NIBLETS, THAT ALARM WAS SENSITIVE!

At midnight, the high-voltage titanium super-reinforced shutters began going **UP** and **DOWN**, making a fur-raising sound. Terrified, I wondered who was there. Then I realized that a pigeon had flown by the window and triggered the alarm.

CHEESE NIBLETS, THAT ALARM WAS SENSITIVE!

I stomped back to bed, but just as my head hit the pillow, the shutters began going **UP** and **DOWN** again, this time because a bus drove past.

When I tried to stop the shutters, they **SLAMMED** down on my tail!

I got up at dawn, totally **EXHAUSTED**.

Scratch . . .

Yawn!

Oops . . .

I shuffled down the hall as the hum of the **CAMERAS** followed my every move.

Hummmmmmmm!

Without paying the **LEAST** attention to the video cameras, I **scratched** my tummy, **STRETCHED**, made a **hippopotamus-sized** yawn, and then (yes, I admit it) PiCKED MY NoSE. After a second, I remembered my manners and stopped. Even though I was all alone, I turned **RED**. Whoops! I was glad no one could see me.

A few minutes later, I turned on the television to catch the morning news. The **TV** commentator announced, "And now an exclusive on the life of **WILD APES**!"

A mouse popped up on the screen, in pajamas, **scratching** his tummy, **STRETCHING**, yawning, and **PICKING** his nose.

Rancid rat hairs, that mouse was me!

I **GASPED** in horror, staggered in shock, and flushed with embarrassment. They had aired my every action recorded by the antitheft cameras! I grabbed the phone to

complain to the mice at **SAFE SQUEAK**, but after ten rings, their answering machine kicked on.

"Our office is closed. Please leave a message or call back when we're open."

Beeeeeeeeeeeeeeeeeep!

I was so angry, **steam** poured out of my ears.

While I waited for the office to open, I *Grrrr...* decided to cheer myself up by making a yummy breakfast.

I looked at the TV screen again as the TV reporter sputtered, "We apologize for the **technical difficulties**. . . . We now return you to our **regularly** scheduled program on wild apes!"

But instead of monkeys, the

SCREEN showed Belinda Fuzzypaws, the mayor's wife, with **rollers** in her fur! She was followed by Samantha Tattletail, the gossip reporter, in a bathrobe with cucumber slices on her eyes!

Finally, Sally Ratmousen, the publisher of *The Daily Rat* (and my rival), was shown exercising in a ridiculous **PINK** tutu!

I have to admit that I **cracked** up when I saw Sally in her tutu. But then I remembered the shots of me picking my nose, and stopped laughing. Just like the video

of me, I bet that footage was from Sally's new **SAFE SQUEAK** antitheft camera. *But why was it on TV?* I thought as I put cereal in a bowl, then poured in lots of milk. I love soggy cereal!

As I was pouring, a little paper boat emerged from the carton. How did it get there? And more important,  **who put it there**?

I picked it up and noticed a little note **rolled up** inside it. It was another message from 00K!

> 00G, open the door and get out immediately! Hey, what are you waiting for? I said now!
>
> Sincerely, 00K
>
> P.S.: Destroy this message after you read it. But don't eat it! It's made of paper!

My heart began to race. WHY did I have to get out of my house? Was it going to BLOW up? Was someone watching me?

I decided I wasn't taking any chances. I TORE up the note. Then I ran outside.

M.I.S.S.O.

Parked in front of my house was a super-long, **DARK** limousine. It had **DARK**-tinted windows and was driven by a driver dressed in a **DARK** uniform.

Just then the door sprang open and a mechanical arm **GRABBED** me by my pajamas, lifted me up, and pulled me into the car.

Terrified, I squeaked, "**Heeeeeelp!**

Let me out! I can't come — I'm in my pajamas!"

But before I knew it, the door had closed behind me with a loud **CLICK**!

I knocked on the glass panel that separated me from the driver.

"Please stop! I told you, I can't come — I'm in my pajamas!"

The driver answered with an **EERIE** robotic voice.

"SOR-RY, MIS-TER STIL-TON, THE ROUTE

HAS BEEN SET. IT IS NOT POSS-I-BLE TO MO-DI-FY IT."

A wave of **panic** spread through me. Why wouldn't this crazy driver open the door? What if someone saw me in my pj's? How **embarrassing**! I'd never live it down!

"Please!" I squeaked again. "I'm in my pajamas!"

The driver paid no attention. "SOR-RY MIS-TER STIL-TON, THE ROUTE HAS BEEN SET. IT IS NOT POSS-I-BLE TO MO-DI-FY IT," he repeated.

Then he turned his head toward me. I let out a loud **squeak**! He had turned his head 180 degrees!

It was then that I realized something truly **TERRIFYING**. The driver wasn't a real mouse at all. He was a **Robot**!

I gulped. Oh, how did I end up in these **fUP-PaiSiNG** situations?

"Let me out!" I insisted.

But nothing happened. Instead my driver said, *"SOR-RY MIS-TER STIL-TON, THE ROUTE HAS BEEN SET. SEC-RET MIS-SION IS A-BOUT TO COM-MENCE IN FIVE SEC-ONDS . . . FOUR . . . THREE . . . TWO . . . ONE . . ."*

CLICK!

Just then words flashed on a screen in front of my seat.

URGENT MESSAGE FOR 00G FROM 00K

Stop screaming!

You're on a secret mission!

Get control of yourself. Put on the clothes that are under the seat. (See, now you don't have to be embarrassed about those silly pj's!)

Our secret automated transportation system will take you directly to M.I.S.S.O. headquarters.

M.I.S.S.O., as in Mouse Island Secret Service Organization, but also as in Move It, Scaredy-Snout, Or else!

I did as I was told.

In just a few minutes, I was out of my **cheese**-slice pj's and dressed in a trench coat and bow tie. I must say, I was feeling pretty cool.

I mean, I know that they say, "Clothes don't

SOME SPECIAL SECRET AGENT GADGETS

Bow tie: when loosened, becomes a rope

Binoculars/glasses: double as night-vision goggles

Belt: doubles as a harness for a quick getaway

Wristwatch: with micro-movie projector

Shoe heels: with hidden lock-picking tools

Video phone: with X-ray viewer

Shoe soles: soundproof and antigravity

Anticat signal that detects feline whereabouts

Case of very pesky micro-fleas

Anticat vest

Pocket inflatable boat

Chamomile-concentrate sleeping powder

Fountain pen with microphone

Ring with sneezing powder

make the mouse," but as soon as I put on
my **SECRET AGENT** clothes, I felt better:

STRONGER!   SMARTER!

TALLER!

AND MUCH, MUCH,
MUUUUUUCH MORE
COURAGEOUS!

I checked my appearance
in the rearview mirror.

"Not bad," I said to
myself as I adjusted my
bow tie.

I was practicing a sly
WINK and feeling confident when the

Not bad!

limo **screeched** to a stop. I was catapulted toward the front.

"Hey, watch it!" I cried.

Watch it!

Unfazed, the driver answered, "*SOR-RY MIS-TER STIL-TON, THE ROUTE HAS BEEN SET. IT IS NOT POSS-I-BLE TO MO-DI-FY IT. END OF RIDE. GOOD-BYE!*"

Without warning, the seat belt **UNBUCKLED** and the mechanical arm grabbed me by the jacket and threw me in a bin filled with **stinky** garbage. The bottom of the garbage bin opened and I fell *down, down, down*. . . .

Help!

A Secret Is a Secret. . . .

I *slid* down a strange transparent plastic tube for what seemed like forever, until I landed on my tail on a very **HARD** marble floor. **BANG!**

Youch! That hurt!

Judging from the stench of fish and from

the bin full of **smelly** bones, I figured I was somewhere under New Mouse City's port. I can't tell you more than that — otherwise, what kind of *SECRET AGENT* would I be? A secret is a secret. . . .

I started wiping **stinky** garbage off my coat and picking it out of my fur when I noticed the room was full of rodents all dressed like me. That's right, they were all *SECRET AGENTS*!

I was in M.I.S.S.O.'s secret headquarters!

One of the rodents had **HUGE** square shoulders, **STRONG** muscular arms, and, of course, was wearing his DARK sunglasses. I recognized him immediately. It was my friend Kornelius von Kickpaw. Otherwise known as 00K!

Kornelius shot me a small smile. Or was it a smirk?

I **shook** his paw.

"It's great to see you, Korneli . . . ahem . . . I mean, OOK!" I stammered. Then I noticed the mouse standing next to him and my fur turned beet **red**. It was his charming sister, OOV.

Before I could say hello, OOK shook my paw, almost **CRUSHING** it. "Welcome, OOG. But enough with the small talk. Let's get to work!" he said.

Everyone sat around a CRYSTAL table facing a gigantic screen. At the head of the table sat M.I.S.S.O.'s **CHIEF** secret agent.

"The situation is grave — very grave," he said in a **serious** tone.

Everyone nodded.

I started to nod, too, but then I realized I had **NO IDEA** what he was talking about. So I asked timidly, "Why, what happened?"

OOA   OOC   OOS   OOH

The whole room turned and looked at me as if I had two **snouts**. The chief just laughed. "Very funny, 00G," he said with a wink. "Of course you know I am talking about the wave of **thefts** in the city and the strange antitheft satellite devices that have been planted everywhere. Something terrible is **TERRORIZING** New Mouse City!"

As soon as I heard those words, I started to shake with fright.

"**We have to do something right away!**" I squeaked.

We have to do something right away!

OOT   OOF   OOO   OOB

Suddenly, the enormouse plasma screen in front of us turned on. A masked, **MENACING**, ugly figure appeared.

"Rodents of New Mouse City, you're in my power!" the figure declared in a deep, **EVIL** voice. "I can **control** all the alarm systems, all the information, and all the communication systems in New Mouse City from my secret satellite! And don't bother trying to look for it. **YOU'LL NEVER FIND IT!**"

I started to feel worried, but the figure wasn't done talking. "You have **ONE** week to get me a mountain of solid GOLD coins. And that mountain better be as tall as a skyscraper . . . or there'll be **TROUBLE**!"

Then he burst out in a chilling laugh. **"MWAHAHA!"**

The screen faded to B L A C K as his laughter died. The chief announced, "Ladies and gentlemice, as *FEARLESS DOG* said, we have to do something right away. Who wants to go with him?"

FEARLESS
00G

I **PUFFED** up my fur with pride. **FEARLESS 00G.** Nobody had ever called me that before! But then I remembered what the chief had said about me going somewhere. I had a feeling he wasn't talking about a trip to **THE SLICE RAT**, my favorite pizza place.

Just then 00K exclaimed, "I'll go with him!"

An instant later, I Smelled a sweet perfume. It was 00V's! She sat next to me and declared, "I'll go, too!"

I was about to ask where we were going when the chief agent rose and said, "Great! It's all settled, then! You'll leave

as soon as you've finished training. The **LAUNCH** is expected in exactly **THIRTY-SIX HOURS**. Good luck!"

With that, he pressed a button, and before I knew what was happening, our chairs began to sink **underneath** the floor!

We landed in a **STRANGE** room filled with **STRANGE** machines. A tall mouse greeted us.

"I'm Professor **Astrofur**, and this is my assistant, **Minifur**. We'll be in charge of your training for the LAUNCH. Just step over here. . . ."

"W-w-what launch?" I squeaked, looking around **WILDLY** for an exit.

00K **rolled** his eyes.

"Please, don't embarrass me," he said. "Remember, you're a *M.I.S.S.O.* agent now! (M.I.S.S.O. as in: *M*ove *I*t, *S*caredy-*S*nout, *O*r else!)"

I **cringed**. "I prefer *M.I.S.S.O.* as in: *M*aybe *I* *S*hould *S*camper *O*ut of here!" I wailed.

Just then I realized the **CHARMING** 00V was staring at me. I tried to remember

the confident expression I had in front of the mirror the day before, when I felt like a **REAL HERO**. But I couldn't.

Professor Astrofur smiled and said, "Of course, 00G, let me explain. I'm talking about your LAUNCH on the spaceship **RATOLLO 16**. All you have to do is find and disable the satellite that the EVIL masked rodent is using to control New Mouse City. And don't worry — you have exactly thirty-five hours and fifty-five minutes before the launch. The countdown starts now!"

I would have **CRIED**, but instead I passed out.

Ack!

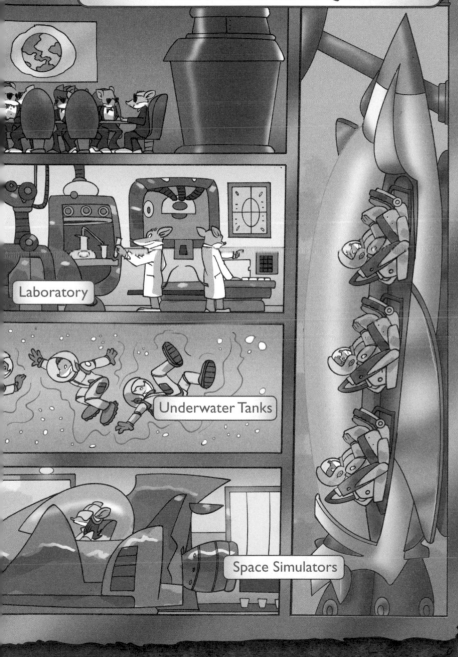

I'M A HOPELESS CASE!

I quickly opened my eyes, because 00K was **SLAPPING** me silly while 00V fanned me with her **SCENTED** handkerchief.

"You can do it, 00G!" 00V insisted. "Just think of all those poor rodents who are in **DANGER**! It's up to us to help them!"

00V was right! Even though my heart was **pounding** out of my fur, I had to pull myself together.

I got up with my head **spinning**.

Then I said, "Okay, I'm ready! What do I have to do?"

The professor grabbed my sleeve and **DRAGGED** me away before I changed my mind.

"Okay, 00G, come along!" he said. "You'll be starting a **SUPER**-concentrated program of **SUPER** training to become a **SUPER** astronaut!!"

"B-but . . . what about them?" I stammered.

"They're already trained," he explained.

And that's when the **PROBLEMS** began. . . .

First, they gave me a medical exam. I was surrounded by a bunch of rodents in **WHITE COATS** who examined me from the top of my ears to the tip of my tail. Afterward, they shook their heads and whispered in astonishment,

"Wow . . . he's a **mess**!"

"Ugh . . . I wonder if he'll **MAKE** it!"

"Squeak . . . what a **disaster**!"

A doctor came bounding in the room, waving the results of my exam.

"Gentlemice, the results are clear. Agent

00G is a **complete mess**. . . . He's a **HOPELESS CASE**!" he declared.

At that point, I tried to make a quick getaway.

"Did you hear that?" I screeched. "I'm a **HOPELESS CASE**! I don't have what it takes to be an **astronaut**! So, adios, hasta la vista, see you later, and thanks to all!"

But the professor grabbed me by the tail.

"Where do you think you're going?" he

The doctors stared at me with horrified expressions.

They wanted me to swallow a pill that was almost bigger than me!

said. "The chief says we have to get you in **shape** and ship you into SPACE! And no one argues with the chief. Don't worry, we'll fix you up!"

And, boy, did they **fix me up**! They made me swallow a gigantic pill and a protein-rich **shake**. They even gave me a vitamin injection with a huge syringe. I screamed so **loud**, they must have heard me all the way up on Mars!

Then the situation got even worse: I began

Yooouch!

The shake had a disgusting taste!

I ran as fast as I could, but they still got me with the syringe!

the **SUPER-CONCENTRATED** astronaut training. What an absolute and total disaster!

Before I started, the professor explained, "In order to become an astronaut, you must:

- be in excellent **physical shape** (and as far as physiques go, you're in bad shape!)
- have a degree in **SCiENCE** (no creative types needed in space!)
- have an excellent knowledge of **foreign languages** (and made-up languages don't count!)
- not be **afraid** of anything (and I can bet my last cheesecake that you are afraid of everything!)
- have a great capacity to **ADAPT**

Can you do all that?"

"Adapt to what?" I asked.

"Life in space, rookie!" the professor

squeaked. "Oh, and I forgot — it usually takes **three years** to train. But unfortunately you only have **LESS THAN TWO DAYS**, so . . ."

"So?"

"So . . ."

"So, what?"

"So, you've got a right to know — you might not make it back **aLive**!"

I wanted to **SCREAM**. I'm too fond of my fur! But I got distracted when we met 00V in the hall and she exclaimed, "See you in space, 00G! You're a true hero!"

You're a hero!

Hee, hee!

Once again I tried to adopt the expression of a true **HERO**, but all I could manage was a **shaky** smile.

"Y-y-yes, ahem, s-s-see you th-th-there," I stammered. But 00V was already gone.

Oh why, oh why, do I always get tongue-tied around pretty mice?

I stared into the distance until the professor **Pinched** me.

"Wake up! No **TIME** for daydreaming!" he squeaked. "You've got work to do! First you have *12 HOURS* of training in the pool in full gear with your space suit. That's to **TRY** to teach you how to move in space (though you're pretty clumsy). Then you have *12 HOURS* of parabolic flight to **TRY** to get you used to the absence of gravity

MOVING IN SPACE
Moving in space is very different from moving on Earth because of the total absence of gravity. Before leaving Earth, astronauts perform rigorous exercises in underwater tanks to simulate the feeling of weightlessness.

(though you're already pretty slow). Then **8 HOURS** of simulated aerospace piloting to **TRY** to teach you to steer the spaceship (though you're so spastic). And that's it!"

"**THAT'S IT?!**" I screeched. "That schedule is **IMPOSSIBLE**! What about a **dinner** break?"

"No breaks!" the professor said.

"How about **lunch**?" I asked.

"Nope," he insisted.

"A **snack**, maybe, or a little **NAP**?" I pleaded.

"Not a chance!" he responded. "There's no time to waste, rookie! Let's face it, you need all the **training** you can get if the chief wants me to somehow turn you into a **SUPER ASTRONAUT** in thirty-two hours!"

HERE'S MY THIRTY-TWO HOURS OF POWER TRAINING!

1. POOL TRAINING

I had to wear a space suit and repair a fake spaceship while floating in a pool! Slimy Swiss cheese, I felt as awkward as a sewer rat on top of a skyscraper!

2. ZERO-GRAVITY TRAINING ON A PARABOLIC FLIGHT

I took a crazy flight on a plane! It flew upward, then the pilot turned off the engine, the plane went into a free fall, and I began to float weightlessly. Then the pilot turned the engine back on and the plane flew up again to repeat the cycle. Eeek — I have a weak stomach!

3. SIMULATING FLIGHT

I had to simulate piloting a spaceship for eight solid hours! The training program felt like a very complicated video game where I had to control a spaceship. At one point, I was even hit by a fake shower of asteroids. Yikes!

THE ROOM IS SPIIIIIIINNNING! CHEESE NIBLETS!

BLASTOFF!

Thirty-two hours later, the professor squeaked, "Okay, no more training. It's SHOWTIME!"

Completely panicked, I **WHINED**, "But I'm not ready! Can't I train some more? Maybe for another . . . two or three HUNDRED years?"

The professor *snorted*.

"Nice try," he said. "Now get moving! It's three hours until takeoff!"

Whiskers **shaking**, I hurried to the subterranean launching pad to meet 00K and 00V.

They were surrounded by all of the *M.I.S.S.O.* agents and the chief.

"Agent 00G, we expect a lot from you. Go

and return **VICTORIOUS**!" he bellowed.

For the third time, I tried to remember what the expression of a real **HERO** looked like. But I couldn't.

Even so, I didn't want to embarrass myself in front of the charming OOV, so I said, "I will do my best, sir!"

I boarded **RATOLLO 16**, took my seat, and buckled my seat belt.

While the experts were finishing the last check before takeoff, I tried to remain calm. *This is nothing*, I told myself. *It's just like a ride at an amousement park.* Too bad I hate amousement parks!

After **ONE HOUR**, my head was **pounding** from the stress.

After **TWO HOURS**, my stomach began Flip-flopping like my cousin Springtail on a trampoline.

After **THREE HOURS**, I was such a bundle of nerves I couldn't even remember my own name!

Holey cheese! Those were the longest **THREE HOURS** of my life!

Finally, from mission control, the chief ordered, "Crew, lock your helmets and put down your visors! Activate all systems. Ignition on. **BLASTOFF!**"

There was a great **ROAR**. The superspeed acceleration crushed us against the seats.

"Let me *ooooooffffffff*!" I squeaked.

"Sorry, 00G." 00K smirked. "You're in until the **end** of the mission. That is, if we're still **alive** at the end."

00V nodded. "Speaking of the **END**, 00G, have you written down your last wishes?"

she asked. "I mean, if you do croak, do you want a fancy funeral? How about a nice **marble** statue of you dressed up like an astronaut?"

"**Marble** would be nice," I said. "You know, I wouldn't want anything cheap like plastic." Then I thought about what we were discussing and felt **queasy**.

I gripped the arms of the seat. My head was

spinning . . .
spinning . . .
spinning. . . .

I didn't move a muscle for **A THOUSAND HOURS**. Well, okay, maybe it wasn't that long, but you get the idea.

Then I heard OOK **TAPPING** my helmet.

"Knock, knock . . . anybody there? I've

got good news! We're in **orbit**!" he squeaked.

I opened one eye and saw 00K and 00V **FLOATING** effortlessly in the cockpit!

"Look, 00G! Isn't this an **AWESOME** sight?!" 00V exclaimed.

I unbuckled my seat belt and **Floated** over to her. Even though I was still scared, when 00V held my paw I immediately felt better. Together we stared out the window at the most **beautiful** sight I have ever seen . . . **planet Earth**!

It's hard to describe how I felt up in space. I felt so small compared to the **immense** universe. I also felt so lucky to have all of my family and friends who were way down in **New Mouse City**.

Right then I made a promise to myself. I would try my best to not be a scaredy-mouse, and to **HELP** with this mission.

THE SOLAR SYSTEM
The solar system is made up of eight planets that revolve around the sun: Mercury, Venus, Earth, Mars, Jupiter, Saturn, Uranus, and Neptune. There are more than 140 known moons, ranging in size, that orbit around many of these planets.

And that, of course, meant stopping the **EVIL RODENT** who was terrorizing the mice of New Mouse City!

I smiled at OOK and OOV. Even though they are **supercool** mice, I could tell they were also impressed with our **amazing** view of the solar system.

"This calls for a toast!" declared OOK. "Let's have a snack now, and in a few minutes we'll start **dancing**."

I gulped. I wasn't much of a dancer. I hoped I wouldn't **embarrass** myself in front of OOV.

Meanwhile, OOK handed out boxes of cheddar **CRACKERS**, condensed mozzarella **milkshakes**, and freeze-dried **CHEESECAKE**.

I was starving. But when I pulled the lid off the shake, it floated out of my paws and *spilled* all over the place!

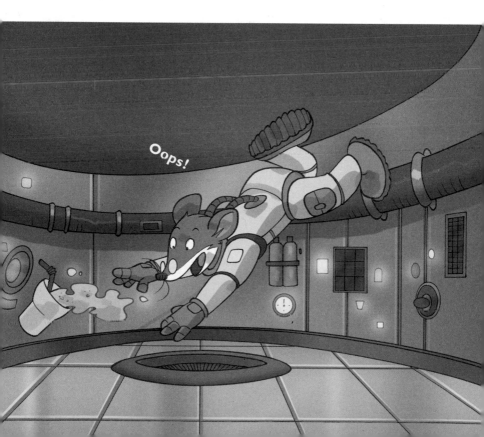

I Told You We'd Be Dancing!

After I chased my shake down and gobbled some freeze-dried cheesecake, I began to relax. Maybe this space thing wasn't so hard after all. I was getting used to FLOATING. And the view was so spectacular it left me **squeakless**!

At that moment, I felt as if I could do anything. I wondered when 00K was going to start the music. Maybe I was underestimating my dancing abilities. Who knows? 00V might even be impressed!

I was thinking I could try out some cool moves I'd seen once in a music video. But suddenly, something *crashed* into our spaceship!

My head hit the wall with a loud **SMACK**. Youch!

After the first collision, there was another and another. . . .

"Everyone to your station!" OOK hollered. "We're in the middle of a **massive swarm** of asteroids.* I told you we'd be dancing!"

* *Asteroids* are small rocky bodies traveling in space. They are found primarily between the orbits of Mars and Jupiter.

Yikes! What a **DANCE**! We were bounced around the ship like Ping-Pong balls.

As soon as we could reach our seats, we buckled our seat belts and tried to make contact with **M.I.S.S.O.** secret headquarters.

"**RATOLLO 16** here. **RATOLLO 16** calling Earth. Do you read me? Over."

But the only thing we heard was "This is Earth . . . *bzzzzzz bzzzz . . . bzzzzzz . . .* **DANGER** . . . *bzzzz . . .* Over . . . *Bzzzt!*"

We didn't understand a thing. Well, anything except for the word *danger*! After that the signal went **DEAD**.

I was so scared my teeth were chattering up a storm. And for the first time since I knew him, even 00K looked *worried*.

"Communication has been INTERRUPTED," he said. "The transmission went BAD.

From now on, we won't be able to receive instructions from the base. . . ."

I chewed my whiskers. "Wh-what do you mean?" I stammered. "Do you mean that we're **ALONE**? Ab-b-b-andoned in space?"

OOK avoided my eyes. Then he said, "Well, we're not exactly **ALONE** — we just won't be able to ask the base how to get to the **EVIL** rodent's satellite. So we'll have to work **independently** to find and deactivate it before that cheesebrain takes over all of New Mouse City!"

I tried not to burst out **SOBBING**. What did OOK take me for? Even the slowest rodent on the block knew that working **ALONE** and working **independently** meant the exact same thing!

I forced myself to breathe deeply and remain **CALM**.

Suddenly, I had a thought.

"Why can't someone go out and try to repair the communication system?" I asked.

"GREAT IDEA!" 00V exclaimed. "You could go out and repair it while 00K and I manually pilot the ship."

Immediately, my paws began shaking. When I said SOMEONE could repair the system, I hadn't been squeaking about Yours Truly!

But what could I do? The entire fate of New Mouse City was in my PAWS!

Before I could talk myself out of it, I put on my space suit, grabbed some tools, and floated off into deep space to fix the damaged antenna. Only a safety cable kept me tied to the ship. From inside, 00K gave me directions. . . .

"A little **HiGHeR** . . . more to the RIGHT . . . a little to the **LEFT** . . . that's it, you got it! Just remember to move slowly. And whatever you do, don't unhook the cable from the ship. If you do, you'll be *lost in space* forever!"

Lost in space? I tried not to think about it.

Instead I concentrated on the **ANTENNA**. I could already see that the mechanical arm that directed it was dented. It didn't seem too hard to fix. I'd just hit it with a hammer and be on my way.

But just then I ran out of cable. I would have to **unhook** myself to reach the antenna. Very carefully, I detached the cable from the ship and tied it to the base of the antenna. Then I **HIT** it with the hammer . . . and before I knew what was

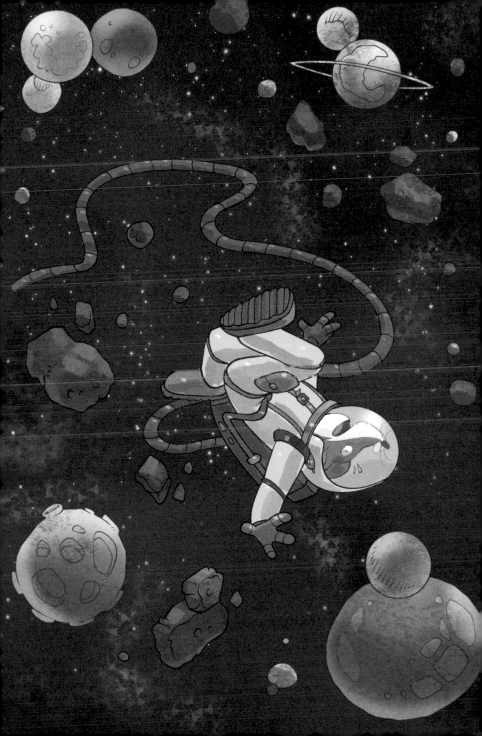

happening, I lost my grip and **plunged into space**!

In the window of **RATOLLO 16**, I could see my friends' **horrified** faces watching me.

Why aren't they coming after me? I thought.

Then I remembered 00K and 00V were trying to operate the **SPACESHIP** without the computer's help. Maybe they weren't able to turn it around.

Plus, my friends couldn't ask **Earth** for help. Oh, what a disaster! I wondered if my **HAMMERING** had even been enough to fix the damaged antenna.

Probably not. Now we were all **doomed**!

Within two minutes, I was *sobbing* away like a newborn mouselet. I cried until my astronaut's helmet filled with tears. It looked like my little fish Hannibal's crystal bowl!

Just then I felt myself being pulled by a **STRANGE** force toward an asteroid the color of **CHEE/E**. How **weird**!

WAIT A MINUTE!

I got closer and closer to the asteroid until my tail **HIT** something hard. **SMACK!** Somehow the strange force had **sucked** me right onto the surface of the asteroid!

How could such a small asteroid have such a **STRONG** force of gravity? At the time, I didn't pay much attention to it. I was just very **happy** to feel a hard surface under my paws instead of **DRIFTING** away in space aimlessly!

In fact, I was so happy, I bent to kiss the surface of that **strange**

THE FORCE OF GRAVITY
The force of gravity — that is, the force of attraction — of every object depends directly on its mass — the amount of matter it's made of. So it's quite unusual for an asteroid, which is much smaller than a planet, to have enough gravity to pull Geronimo with such force. There might be something fishy here!

asteroid. As I did so, I made a wish to remain alive. Maybe a passing satellite would spot me and an expedition would be launched to bring me home! You never know.

But then I noticed something strange. Right near me on the surface of the asteroid was a row of bolts!

Wait a minute! This wasn't a real asteroid. It was completely ARTIFICIAL!

I began to get excited. Maybe this thing was actually a spaceship DiSGUiSeD as an asteroid. Maybe there was **FOOD** on board (I was starving!), and a communication system so I could send out an **SOS.**

Maybe, just maybe, I'd be **saved**!

Cautiously, I started to EXPLORE the fake asteroid. After a few steps, I fell snout-first into a hole and *zipped* down a dark tunnel.

I *BOUNCED* down a short ramp, ending up in what looked like a warehouse filled with boxes and strange machinery.

"Youch!"

I was massaging my bruised tail when a **SLIDING** door

opened before me and a robot grabbed me with its mechanical arm. It dragged me away, croaking, *"IN-TRU-DER CAUGHT AND IM-PRIS-ONED!"*

It threw me inside a round room where two rodents were working in front of an **ENORMOUSE** screen.

"Thank you, **R-51**. You can go now," said a rodent. Then he turned toward me.

"Well, lookie who the cat dragged in thanks to our **SUPER GRAVITATIONAL SIMULATOR**!" he sneered.

When he turned toward me, I recognized him immediately. It

What's going on?

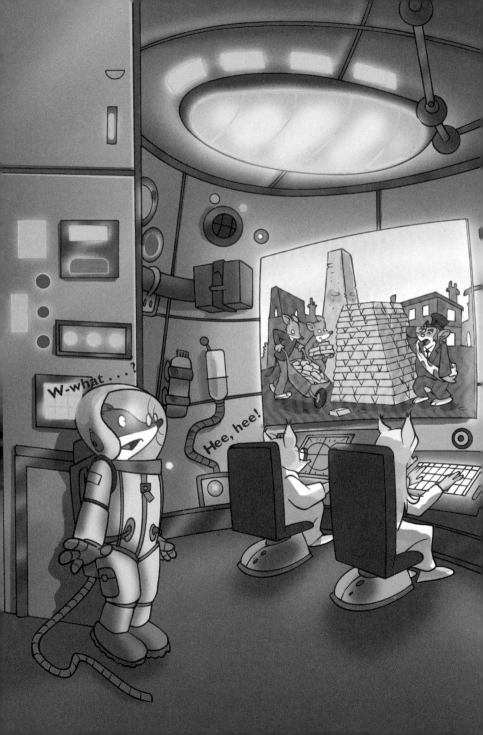

was the same rodent who had appeared on the screen at **M.I.S.S.O.** headquarters, demanding a pile of GOLD and threatening to take over the city! Next to him sat Suzy Slyrat, the mouse who had sold me the **SAFE SQUEAK** device.

"So you are the two cheesebrains who broke into my home!" I shrieked. "How **DARE** you!"

"The name's **Dr. Wicked Whiskers**. But everyone just calls me Dr. Wicked," the mouse announced. "And you can scream all you want, but it won't help. My **genius** plan is almost done. First I terrorized New Mouse City's rodents with a series of robberies, then I sold them satellite antitheft devices from **SAFE SQUEAK**. Once I did that, I gained control of all the computers in New Mouse City. In exactly **TWENTY-TWO**

hours and **FIFTEEN** minutes, I'll land in New Mouse City and pick up the mountain of GOLD that your foolish friends put together for me. But that's not all. **LOOK!**"

With a smirk he went to a keyboard and typed a series of numbers and letters. A second later, words appeared on the screen:

> *MEGAVORTEX ACTIVATED*
> *REMAINING TIME: 24 HOURS*

"As soon as I have escaped with my mountain of GOLD, the MegaVortex will clean out all New Mouse City's bank accounts and **destroy** all communication and information systems. That way, I'll have a clean getaway. Oh, I almost forgot. In twenty-four hours and thirty minutes, you will be **PULVERIZED**, and I'll be rich, very rich!"

Suzy Slyrat grinned. "Daddy, you're a **genius**!" she squeaked, kissing him on the snout.

"Thanks!" **Dr. Wicked** chuckled as he ticd my legs so I couldn't run. Just then a robotic voice rang out in the room,

"AU-TO SAT-EL-LITE DE-STRUC-TION IN TWEN-TY-FOUR HOURS, E-LEV-EN MIN-UTES, THIR-TY SEC-ONDS!"

SOS

The robotic voice continued to ring out at regular intervals, making me **SQUIRM** each time. Oh, how did I get myself into such a **mess**? I had to do something, and fast!

Suddenly, I had a fabumouse idea. I began **POUNDING** against the metal walls.

BANG BANG BANG
BANG . . . BANG . . . BANG . . .
BANG BANG BANG

Three short sounds, then three long, then three short. It was the **SOS** message in Morse code,* a distress signal for help.

I continued sending my message for hours and hours. Finally, exhausted, I **SANK** to the ground and fell asleep.

---

* *Morse code* is a system of communicating textual information with an alphabet of dots, dashes, and spaces. It is transmitted with a series of on-off tones or lights.

No one could hear me.

I was all alone.

Alone in deep space.

I tossed and turned and had terrible **NIGHTMARES**. I even dreamed that a Martian was tapping my forehead with its **slimy** tentacles. . . .

TAP, TAP! TAP, TAP!

The **tapping** continued on my forehead until I woke up with a start. Was this it? Was this the end? Was I about to be eaten by a

Tap, tap!

ferocious Martian? But when I opened my eyes, instead of a Martian, I saw OOK and OOV. Was I still dreaming?

I **PINCHED** myself to make sure. "Youch!" I wailed. That hurt!

I could hardly believe it. I wasn't dreaming! I wasn't going to be **Martian meat** after all. My **FRIENDS** had come to save me!

I jumped up. OOK cut the ROPE tying me.

Tap, tap!

"How did you find me?" I squeaked.

"It was all thanks to you, Geronimo. You **repaired** the antenna! The base was able to communicate the position of that cheesebrain's **SATELLITE**, and we came immediately. We thought you were a goner!" 00K explained, looking away.

I could tell he was *choked* up. Even though 00K is a **TOUGH** mouse, he's a real softy at heart.

00V went on with the story, grinning from ear to ear.

"As we were exploring the satellite, we heard someone **TAPPING** at regular intervals. We knew it had to be an **SOS**! Then we just followed the **signal** and . . . here we are!"

I was so happy I almost forgot we were still in **danger**. Just then a robotic voice announced, *"AU-TO SAT-EL-LITE DE-STRUC-TION IN FOUR HOURS AND ZE-RO MIN-UTES, ZE-RO SEC-ONDS!"*

Sadly, I explained the situation.

"We're **doomed**." I sighed.

But 00K CLAPPED me on the back. "Don't be so pessimistic, Agent 00G," he said with a teasing smile. "After all, we are from ***M.I.S.S.O.*** (as in ***M***ouse, ***I S***wear, ***S***uck it up ***O***r else!)."

My friend was right. No use getting discouraged.

"Well, what are we waiting for?" I said, returning 00K's Smile. "Let's go!"

00V sprang into action. "Leave the MEGAVORTEX to me. I'll take care of deactivating the program. I don't mean to **BRAG**, but I'm the best programmer in all of M.I.S.S.O."

Then she sat down at the computer and started tapping away.

Meanwhile, 00K and I went to find and deactivate the **auto-destruction** device. But we couldn't locate it.

Rat-munching rattlesnakes! What a PICKLE we were in!

Just thinking about **PICKLES** made my stomach growl. I was starving. *I'd give my left paw for a nice bowl of* MAC AND CHEESE*!* I thought. Well, okay, maybe I wouldn't really give away my paw. But you get the idea.

There was no time to think about food, though. We only had **ONE HOUR** left!

We went back inside, hoping 00V had had better **LUCK**, but she looked upset.

"It's almost done, but there's a BLOCK. I need the **PASSWORD** . . . but I don't know what it is!" she cried.

Just then I took a step forward and

accidentally **TRIPPED** over my own feet. I lost my balance and **thrashed** my paws around like a windmill before falling onto a **swivel** chair.

It felt like I'd just been shot out of a **CANNON** as I catapulted on the chair across the room! I rolled forward and landed snout-down on the keyboard in front of 00V. She jumped up with a squeak. "Aaahh!"

"Oops . . ." I whispered.

The computer

buzzed, **"Bzzz! Bzzz! Bzzz!"**

Flashing words appeared across the screen:

MEGAVORTEX PROGRAM
DEACTIVATED

I couldn't believe my eyes. Somehow, when my snout **smacked** into the keyboard, I had pressed the right keys for the password!

The **MEGAVORTEX** program was deactivated. Dr. Wicked's plan had failed! New Mouse City was **safe**!

We were just starting to celebrate when a robotic voice rang out in the room.

"AU-TO SAT-EL-LITE DE-STRUC-TION IN ZE-RO HOURS, FIF-TEEN MIN-UTES, ZE-RO SEC-ONDS!"

00K pushed us toward the door.

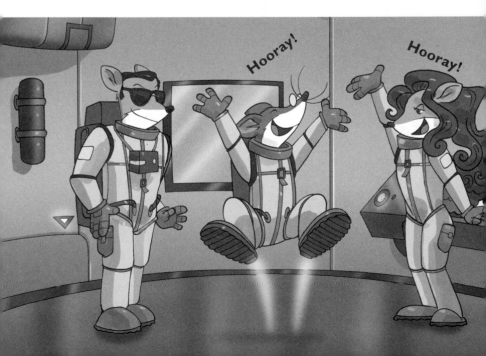

"The auto-destruction program was not **DEACTIVATED**! We need to get out of here right away!" he instructed. "Everyone to the spaceship! *NOW!*"

JUST IN TIME!

We rushed out of the computer room toward **RATOLLO 16**. Fortunately, the fake **ASTEROID** was small and we didn't have to go too far.

Inside the **SPACESHIP**, we quickly turned on the ignition and left.

In a few minutes, we were far away from the **CHEESE**-colored satellite.

HOLEY CHEESE! We left just in time! We watched the tremendous **EXPLOSION** in horror. The satellite blew up into a million **tiny** pieces, like Parmesan flakes in the sky.

It was then that I realized that those tiny pieces could have been us.

I was so relieved I let out a **HUGE** sigh

and then . . . I fainted.

I came to soon after, and found myself belted to my seat. 00V was fanning me with her **scented** hanky.

"Wow, 00G! You are a real **HERO**!" she exclaimed.

I was so embarrassed, my fur turned three shades of **red**.

"Ahem, well actually, I'm really a scaredy-mouse," I said. "And I just fainted. A real **HERO** isn't afraid of anything."

"Not true," 00K insisted, **FLOATING** up to us. "Everyone gets afraid, 00G. But when we are able to conquer our **fears**, we are true heroes. And thanks to your heroic efforts, we were able to **SAVE** New Mouse City!"

Just then I noticed the **SPACESHIP'S** TV screen. It was playing that night's news.

A video showed a close-up of **Dr. Wicked** and Suzy fleeing the city.

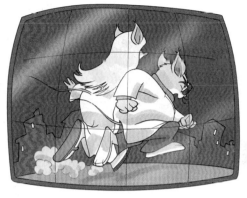

"**Breaking news!** The two cheesebrains who have been burglarizing our fair city have left the island! Yes, folks, your GOLD is safe again!" the announcer reported.

"Reliable sources tell us credit goes to M.I.S.S.O.'s unknown **HEROES**. From all of us here at **WRAT TV**, we'd like to extend our sincerest thanks!"

Just then **Professor Astrofur** appeared on the screen.

"Congrats, rookie!" He beamed. "I really didn't think you could do it. I've never trained anyone who seemed like such a **hopeless** case!"

Then M.I.S.S.O.'s **chief** appeared. "*Thank you*, mice! Mission accomplished!" he squeaked. "We are **PROUD** of you, especially 00G. I never thought you'd make it out of this mission *alive*! Now, I would like you to open up the secret door marked **A.W.T.E.W.**"

Immediately, I began to **PANIC**. What did **A.W.T.E.W.** mean? I hoped it wasn't

another **scary** mission. I was so tired. I was dying to get home to my **COZY** mouse hole.

"Ahem, excuse me, Chief — why do we have to open the door?" I asked. "Honestly, I was hoping to go home, relax, and get rid of all those noisy **SAFE SQUEAK** antitheft devices."

The chief grinned. "Don't worry, 00G. We had them removed. Now open the door!" he insisted.

With **trembling** paws, I pushed the button above the marked door. I heard a **CLICK** . . . then three mechanical arms shot out toward our suits, pinning on **ReD CHeDDaR** Medals of Honor as speakers blared New Mouse City's anthem.

What does **A.W.T.E.W.** mean, you ask? I'll tell you. It means "**ALL'S WELL THAT ENDS WELL!**"

In fact, it couldn't have ended better than this. And that's the truth, or my name isn't *Geronimo Stilton*!

Don't miss any of my other fabumouse adventures!

#1 Lost Treasure of the Emerald Eye

#2 The Curse of the Cheese Pyramid

#3 Cat and Mouse in a Haunted House

#4 I'm Too Fond of My Fur!

#5 Four Mice Deep in the Jungle

#6 Paws Off, Cheddarface!

#7 Red Pizzas for a Blue Count

#8 Attack of the Bandit Cats

#9 A Fabumouse Vacation for Geronimo

#10 All Because of a Cup of Coffee

#11 It's Halloween, You 'Fraidy Mouse!

#12 Merry Christmas, Geronimo!

#13 The Phantom of the Subway

#14 The Temple of the Ruby of Fire

#15 The Mona Mousa Code

#16 A Cheese-Colored Camper

#17 Watch Your Whiskers, Stilton!

#18 Shipwreck on the Pirate Islands

#19 My Name Is Stilton, Geronimo Stilton

#20 Surf's Up, Geronimo!

#21 The Wild, Wild West

#22 The Secret of Cacklefur Castle

A Christmas Tale

#23 Valentine's Day Disaster

#24 Field Trip to Niagara Falls

#25 The Search for Sunken Treasure

#26 The Mummy with No Name

#27 The Christmas Toy Factory

#28 Wedding Crasher

#29 Down and Out Down Under

#30 The Mouse Island Marathon

#31 The Mysterious Cheese Thief

Christmas Catastrophe

#32 Valley of the Giant Skeletons

#33 Geronimo and the Gold Medal Mystery

#34 Geronimo Stilton, Secret Agent

#35 A Very Merry Christmas

#36 Geronimo's Valentine

#37 The Race
Across America

#38 A Fabumouse
School Adventure

#39 Singing
Sensation

#40 The Karate
Mouse

#41 Mighty
Mount
Kilimanjaro

#42 The Peculiar
Pumpkin Thief

#43 I'm Not a
Supermouse!

#44 The Giant
Diamond Robbery

#45 Save the
White Whale!

#46 The Haunted
Castle

#47 Run for the
Hills, Geronimo!

#48 The Mystery
in Venice

#49 The Way of
the Samurai

#50 This Hotel is
Haunted

#51 The
Enormouse Pearl
Heist

#52 Mouse in
Space!

Up next!

#53 Rumble in
the Jungle

Don't miss these very special editions!

THE KINGDOM OF FANTASY

THE QUEST FOR PARADISE: THE RETURN TO THE KINGDOM OF FANTASY

THE AMAZING VOYAGE: THE THIRD ADVENTURE IN THE KINGDOM OF FANTASY

THE DRAGON PROPHECY: THE FOURTH ADVENTURE IN THE KINGDOM OF FANTASY

Check out my first hardcover!

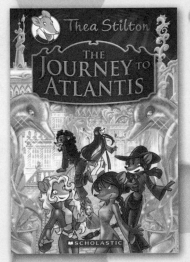

THEA STILTON: THE JOURNEY TO ATLANTIS

Meet
GERONIMO STILTONOOT

He is a cavemouse — Geronimo Stilton's ancient ancestor! He runs the stone newspaper in the prehistoric village of Old Mouse City. From dealing with dinosaurs to dodging meteorites, his life in the Stone Age is full of adventure!

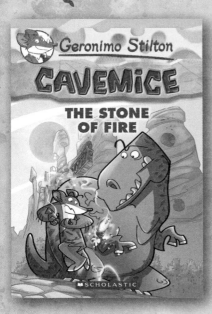

THE STONE OF FIRE

The Stone of Fire — the most precious artifact in the Old Mouse City mouseum — has been stolen! It's up to Geronimo Stiltonoot and his cavemouse friend Hercule Poirat to retrieve the stone from Tiger Khan and his band of fearsome felines.

Be sure to check out these exciting Thea Sisters adventures!

Thea Stilton and the Dragon's Code

Thea Stilton and the Mountain of Fire

Thea Stilton and the Ghost of the Shipwreck

Thea Stilton and the Secret City

Thea Stilton and the Mystery in Paris

Thea Stilton and the Cherry Blossom Adventure

Thea Stilton and the Star Castaways

Thea Stilton: Big Trouble in the Big Apple

Thea Stilton and the Ice Treasure

Thea Stilton and the Secret of the Old Castle

Thea Stilton and the Blue Scarab Hunt

Thea Stilton and the Prince's Emerald

Thea Stilton and the Mystery on the Orient Express

Meet
CREEPELLA VON CACKLEFUR

I, *Geronimo Stilton*, have a lot of mouse
friends, but none as **spooky** as my friend
CREEPELLA VON CACKLEFUR! She is an
enchanting and MYSTERIOUS mouse
with a pet bat named Bitewing.
    YIKES!   I'm a real 'fraidy mouse, but
even I think CREEPELLA and her family are
AWFULLY fascinating. I can't wait for
you to read all about CREEPELLA in these
fa-mouse-ly funny and **spectacularly
spooky** tales!

**#1 THE THIRTEEN
GHOSTS**

**#2 MEET ME IN
HORRORWOOD**

**#3 GHOST PIRATE
TREASURE**

**#4 RETURN OF THE
VAMPIRE**

ABOUT THE AUTHOR

Born in New Mouse City, Mouse Island, **GERONIMO STILTON** is Rattus Emeritus of Mousomorphic Literature and of Neo-Ratonic Comparative Philosophy. For the past twenty years, he has been running *The Rodent's Gazette,* New Mouse City's most widely read daily newspaper.

Stilton was awarded the Ratitzer Prize for his scoops on *The Curse of the Cheese Pyramid* and *The Search for Sunken Treasure.* He has also received the Andersen 2000 Prize for Personality of the Year. One of his bestsellers won the 2002 eBook Award for world's best ratlings' electronic book. His works have been published all over the globe.

In his spare time, Mr. Stilton collects antique cheese rinds and plays golf. But what he most enjoys is telling stories to his nephew Benjamin.

1. Main entrance
2. Printing presses (where the books and newspaper are printed)
3. Accounts department
4. Editorial room (where the editors, illustrators, and designers work)
5. Geronimo Stilton's office
6. Helicopter landing pad

THE RODENT'S GAZETTE

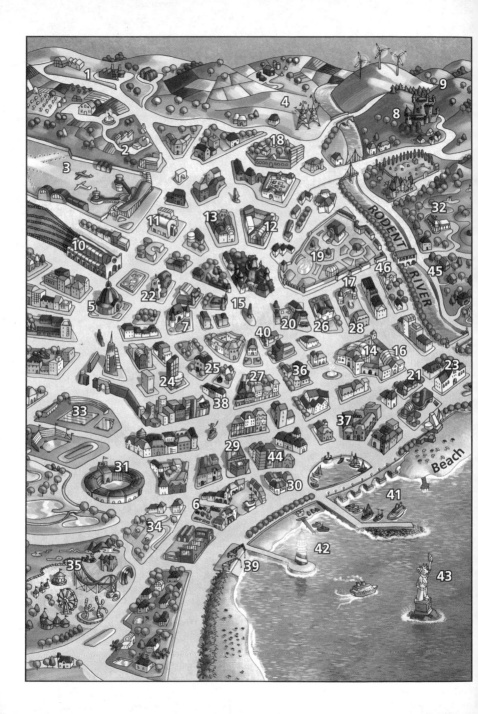

RODENT RIVER

Beach

Map of New Mouse City

1. Industrial Zone
2. Cheese Factories
3. Angorat International Airport
4. WRAT Radio and Television Station
5. Cheese Market
6. Fish Market
7. Town Hall
8. Snotnose Castle
9. The Seven Hills of Mouse Island
10. Mouse Central Station
11. Trade Center
12. Movie Theater
13. Gym
14. Catnegie Hall
15. Singing Stone Plaza
16. The Gouda Theater
17. Grand Hotel
18. Mouse General Hospital
19. Botanical Gardens
20. Cheap Junk for Less (Trap's store)
21. Aunt Sweetfur and Benjamin's House
22. Mouseum of Modern Art
23. University and Library
24. *The Daily Rat*
25. *The Rodent's Gazette*
26. Trap's House
27. Fashion District
28. The Mouse House Restaurant
29. Environmental Protection Center
30. Harbor Office
31. Mousidon Square Garden
32. Golf Course
33. Swimming Pool
34. Tennis Courts
35. Curlyfur Island Amousement Park
36. Geronimo's House
37. Historic District
38. Public Library
39. Shipyard
40. Thea's House
41. New Mouse Harbor
42. Luna Lighthouse
43. The Statue of Liberty
44. Hercule Poirat's Office
45. Petunia Pretty Paws's House
46. Grandfather William's House

Map of Mouse Island

1. Big Ice Lake
2. Frozen Fur Peak
3. Slipperyslopes Glacier
4. Coldcreeps Peak
5. Ratzikistan
6. Transratania
7. Mount Vamp
8. Roastedrat Volcano
9. Brimstone Lake
10. Poopedcat Pass
11. Stinko Peak
12. Dark Forest
13. Vain Vampires Valley
14. Goose Bumps Gorge
15. The Shadow Line Pass
16. Penny Pincher Castle
17. Nature Reserve Park
18. Las Ratayas Marinas
19. Fossil Forest
20. Lake Lake
21. Lake Lakelake
22. Lake Lakelakelake
23. Cheddar Crag
24. Cannycat Castle
25. Valley of the Giant Sequoia
26. Cheddar Springs
27. Sulfurous Swamp
28. Old Reliable Geyser
29. Vole Vale
30. Ravingrat Ravine
31. Gnat Marshes
32. Munster Highlands
33. Mousehara Desert
34. Oasis of the Sweaty Camel
35. Cabbagehead Hill
36. Rattytrap Jungle
37. Rio Mosquito

Dear mouse friends,
Thanks for reading, and farewell
till the next book.
It'll be another whisker-licking-good
adventure, and that's a promise!

Geronimo Stilton